THE

Sarah Jane

ADVENTURES

From the makers of Doctor Who

BBC CHILDREN'S BOOKS

Published by the Penguin Group
Penguin Books Ltd, 80 Strand, London WC2R 0RL, England
Penguin Group (USA) Inc., 375 Hudson Street, New York, New York 10014, USA
Penguin Group (Australia) Ltd, 250 Camberwell Road, Camberwell, Victoria, 3124, Australia
(a division of Pearson Australia Group Pty Ltd)
Canada, India, New Zealand, South Africa

Published by BBC Children's Character Books, 2008
Text and design © Children's Character Books, 2008

10 9 8 7 6 5 4 3 2 1

Sarah Jane Adventures © BBC 2007

www.thesja.com

BBC logo ™ & BBC 1996. Licensed by BBC Worldwide Limited

ISBN 978-1-40590-506-0

Printed in Great Britain by Clays Ltd, St Ives plc

THE Sarah Jane ADVENTURES

From the makers of Doctor Who
Series created by Russell T Davies

The Lost Boy

Written by Gary Russell

Based on the script by Phil Ford

'I saw amazing things, out there in space. But there's strangeness to be found wherever you turn. Life on Earth can be an adventure, too.

You just have to know where to look.'

SARAH JANE SMITH

Chapter One

The nightmare begins

A few months ago, the residents of Hambleton Estate had been a happy lot. The estate had been built in a secluded part of the Lake District, an area that people could move to, to get away from the hustle bustle of cities, of intercity trains and mucky buses. A nice, gentle, new housing development. A place to chill out and relax in.

Which was all fine until the new people moved into Number 64, along with their rusty red van (which might've once belonged to the Royal Mail!), on the corner of the street leading to the park and the road with the fields of ponies and sheep. You see, the people of the estate had moved there from across the UK to escape the drudgery of city life, and they were a friendly lot. They had all got to know one another, sharing shopping trips to Carlisle, running each others kids to school and the cinemas, that sort of thing. So when the new people moved into Number 64 Grass Street, one of the neighbours, Mrs Townsend, made it her business to visit, with a flask of tea, a tray of biscuits – covered in cling-film, naturally, to keep them fresh – and even the traditional bowl of sugar.

But the response had been sullen, almost rude. The newcomers were a couple and their son. The couple were in their early thirties, but had a look that made Mrs Townsend think they were much older. They barely made eye contact, either with her or each other, and the man seemed perpetually angry. Mrs Townsend noticed he had a scar just below the left ear (she noticed things like that) and it crossed her mind he might have got it in a fight – it had that jagged, almost torn look, which such scars do. But she averted her eyes, desperately hoping the man wouldn't notice her gaze, and smiled instead at the woman.

'Thought you might like some tea,' Mrs Townsend started. 'A sort of "Welcome to our neighbourhood" gesture,' she ended, lamely, as the new woman never smiled.

'Thank you,' said the woman, with about as much warmth as an abattoir. 'That's… kind of you.' She smiled and Mrs Townsend thought it was an action she wasn't used to. 'My name is June Goss, this is Marco,' she pointed at her husband. 'We prefer our own company.'

Mrs Townsend wasn't quite sure how to deal with that, but soldiered on, bravely. 'That's nice,' she said. 'Well, if you ever want to chat, you'll find everyone around here friendly enough.'

The back door opened and a boy walked in. As sullen and withdrawn as his parents were, Mrs Townsend could see he was full of life and cheer.

'This place is great, mum,' he said, dropping a football bag on the kitchen floor. 'There are horses and everything down that way, and the bus stop for school is over in the next street and there's a lovely dog in one of the houses and –'

He stopped as he took in Mrs Townsend. 'Oh, hello,' he said. 'I'm Nate.' He politely offered his hand, and Mrs Townsend shook it, relieved that someone in this strange family had a smile.

Nate Goss was about twelve or thirteen years old, Mrs Townsend guessed, and quite rugged, looked like he played a lot of sports. He had mousey brown hair and piercing blue eyes that Mrs Townsend guessed would melt a few hearts in years to come. She glanced at the Everton bag he had put down.

'Local team?'

Nate shook his head. 'Used to live in Guildford, but I learned to love Everton at school.' He looked at his mum. 'My old school.' Then back at Mrs Townsend. 'But I guess my new school here will be good too.' He eased out of the kitchen, pausing only to nick a biscuit from the plate. 'Nice, thanks,' he smiled and was gone. Mrs Townsend noticed a family photo on the sideboard as he passed, showing a grinning Nate clutching a skateboard, his parents stood at either side of him.

Mrs Townsend excused herself from the dour parents and headed home. Such a nice boy - shame about the parents. She wondered what their story was, but guessed she was unlikely to find out. 'Not the chatty types,' she told Mrs Galagher next door, later that day.

Over the next few weeks, the new family made themselves unpopular with the neighbours in a variety of ways. They'd shout at the kids going to and from school. Once, they threw things at a dog, when it was going nowhere near their house. And they called the police to complain about a party held two roads away by a lovely young couple who were making no noise at all. And it was a Friday, so it wasn't as if Marco was working the next day.

During that time, Mrs Townsend gathered that Marco Goss worked in telecommunications and had been transferred up north. His wife stayed at home all day and young Nate was a popular kid at the school, not terribly bright, but a team player, and really good at sports (as she'd guessed) and woodwork. He'd quickly become popular with a lot of the girls at school, and Mrs Townsend wasn't surprised. All of which made his parents' lack of social graces all the more depressing.

It was on a Thursday night, when June Goss had got involved in a particularly heated debate with young Mr Robinson (who was bringing up two daughters by himself after his wife had passed on so tragically young) about dustbins. Specifically, about where they were placed on the street for collection by the binmen. As a result, Mrs Townsend really began to feel quite cross with the new family. The Hambleton estate was about being nice, getting on with your neighbours, and above all, about getting away from aggro and unpleasantness and the Goss' seemed to have brought all their city hang-ups with them from Guildford (which, Mrs Townsend had always believed, was a rather nice place, actually).

At about ten o'clock that night, after dark, Mrs Townsend heard a noise outside in the street. She flicked her curtains apart a smidgen and saw a big truck in the street. Almost as big as a removal truck, but certainly larger than a Transit van. She couldn't really see who was driving, and could only really make out vague shapes. Two adults and a child, a bit on the large size it had to be said, were getting out of the truck.

One of the adults pointed at the Goss' house and all three of them moved up the driveway.

Mrs Townsend switched her lamp off, trying to see the newcomers more clearly, but it didn't help. However, there was something about them, about the way they walked, shuffled in fact, up that driveway, which concerned her. There was definitely something… wrong. That was the only way she could describe it. Wrong.

And then, with a sigh, she let the curtain drop. After all, it was just Goss family business. "We prefer our own company" June had told her, so best to leave them to it.

As Mrs Townsend got ready for bed that night, she was dimly aware of voices (she could recognise Marco Goss' straight away) in the street outside. A couple of shouts followed. Then a brief silence, followed by laughter. She'd never heard either of the adult Goss' laugh before, and it was a strange laugh. Almost mocking. Actually, she wasn't sure if it was the Goss' or the newcomers. As she was halfway up the stairs to bed, she couldn't check the view outside, but by the time she got into her room, she was aware of the sound of the truck driving away followed by the Goss' rusty red van, then nothing else.

It didn't really upset anyone that the Goss family had gone overnight. No one liked them, and at least dogs, kids, parties and Mr Robinson's dustbins were free from their angry moans and grumbles. Nate was missed at school certainly, and Mrs Townsend learned that no one even realised that they had opted to move away. One day they were there, the next they'd gone.

Deep down everyone was a bit relieved. The house was auctioned off not long afterwards and a lovely young couple who liked tea, biscuits, dogs and never objected to dustbin placement moved in a week or two later, and everything went back to normal.

And Mrs Townsend barely gave the Goss family another thought over the next six months, until one Sunday teatime, when she was watching the BBC news with the sound turned down.

And there, on the screen was what looked like June Goss, tearful, animated. Emotional. All the things she'd never really been when living on the Hambleton estate. That was why she turned the volume up, because it seemed so… out of character for her old neighbours.

But she quickly realised she was wrong. These people weren't June and Marco Goss. But they looked terribly similar. How odd, she thought, they look like dead ringers.

Their names were Jay and Heidi Stafford, according to the names flashed up beneath them, and they were appealing for the return of their son, who it seemed had been kidnapped or lost or stolen or something. It crossed Mrs Townsend's mind that something awful had happened to dear Nate – was that why they'd left in a hurry all those months back? But why wait till now to appeal for his return?

Then a photo of the missing boy was flashed up, accompanied by a banner that said ASHLEY STAFFORD – HAVE YOU SEEN HIM?

It wasn't Nate, this was a good looking tall lad, maybe a year or two older, dark hair, bright eyes, thin as a rake. A bit geeky looking, Mrs Townsend thought the phrase was.

A pretty boy, but certainly not Nate Goss.

So, she'd got it wrong, these people looked similar but weren't quite –

And then she stopped and gasped.

Jay Stafford had turned to hug his distraught wife and there, just below his left ear, was a jagged, rough scar.

Now that was weird, Mrs Townsend thought. Not only did they look like the errant Goss parents, but the father had an identical scar to Marco Goss.

Mrs Townsend was wondering what to do, when the doorbell rang.

It was Mr Robinson. One of his girls had torn a skirt and although he could do many things, he explained, sewing wasn't one of them.

And delighted to help a lovely neighbour, Mrs Townsend invited him in and busied around getting her sewing kit out of a cupboard. She casually turned the TV off, all thoughts of missing Goss' people, and missing Stafford boys, out of her mind.

The last image on the TV screen as it powered down was a photo of the missing Ashley Stafford.

A few hundred miles south of Mrs Townsend, and an entire day earlier, Maria Jackson had stared at her father in horror. Well, dismay. Well, shock. Well all right, dismay and shock, but above all, horror.

The weekend before, Alan Jackson had discovered something new about his daughter. All fathers like to think they know their teenage daughters quite well. Few do, obviously, but Alan prided himself on being very much in tune with Maria. This was mainly due to the fact that Alan was a nice guy, liberal, open-minded and really the coolest dad out there. And because he and Maria only had each other. Alan and Chrissie Jackson had separated a year or two earlier, then divorced. That had prompted a relocation, and father and daughter had ended up choosing a house together in Ealing, a pleasant borough on the very border of west London. 36 Bannerman Road, a charming modern two bedroom semi in a quiet neighbourhood. There were shops, parks and a good school, Park Vale. Ealing Broadway was about a twenty minute walk away, central London only about 25 minutes from there by tube.

What Alan Jackson hadn't expected to discover six months or so later was that the lady who lived opposite, Sarah Jane Smith, had secrets. To Alan, Sarah Jane was a journalist, clearly well-off (her house was huge!) and she had adopted a teenager called Luke, who called her 'Mum' and was Maria's best friend. Alan doubted there was anything more than friendship, mainly because Luke was lovely but a bit... weird. Alan once called him a dork, which got Maria very cross and she called Luke adorable. So Alan and Maria had come up with a new phrase for him, 'adorkable', which soon smoothed that problem out.

What Alan had never guessed was that Sarah Jane spent most of her time dealing with aliens from outer space. Nor had he suspected that Luke wasn't an ordinary fourteen year old boy, but had been created by an alien race of would-be conquers called the Bane. That Luke was a genetically-engineered 'superboy', whose amazing intellect was only equalled by his astonishing naïvety, and that he had effectively been born only a few months ago. Alan was also coming to terms with words and phrases such as Slitheen (they were responsible for switching the sun off for a few minutes and had been based at Maria's school), Gorgons (they were responsible for turning him to stone, apparently) and most recently the Trickster, who had sent the world's time-stream into chaos, resulting in firstly Sarah Jane, and then Maria ceasing to exist. It had fallen to Alan, protected by a special alien box it seemed, to save the world. Which he did, just in time to enable Sarah Jane and her amazing sentient computer, Mr Smith (also alien), to divert a meteor that threatened to wipe out all life on Earth when it crashed. Heaven knows what the meteor did after it went spinning off into space, but Alan had been relieved that Sarah Jane had saved the world.

And not for the first time, it transpired.

'Maria,' he was saying, 'Maria, you are fourteen years old.'

'Dad,' she replied, 'without Sarah Jane the world would have died. It's what me and Luke and Clyde do.'

Alan thought of Clyde. Cocky, streetwise and super-cool Clyde, Luke's best friend and as much of an opposite of Luke's reserved geekiness as it was possible to be. Not that Clyde was dim, far from it in fact, but he hated seeming clever and tended to be flippant and a joker and as a result his schoolwork was always a bit behind.

'I'm your father. You never thought I should know about any of this?'

'Like you would've believed me,' she countered. 'Sarah Jane knows what she's doing. She used to work with the Doctor…'

'A man from another world who flies around in space and time, if I remember correctly what you said?'

'Yeah, and now she has a robot dog computer thing called K-9, but he's stopping universal entropy by guarding a black hole or something. And then there's Mr Smith.'

Alan remembered his first encounter with the talking computer, which was built into the chimney stack in Sarah Jane's amazing attic. It had a suave, slightly pompous voice, which was accompanied by weird pulsating, gyrating patterns of light on the screen, which glowed whenever it spoke.

'And which High Street store did he come from? I mean, I know computers, I build programmes for them, and Mr Smith's… well, I'd like to know his specifications, anyway.'

'He's an alien, remember,' Maria said quietly. 'I don't know if Sarah Jane knows exactly where he's from.'

'Right. That fills me with confidence,' Alan said. 'Look, this is serious stuff.'

'You're not going to tell Mum, are you?'

Alan snorted. That was something he and Maria could agree on. 'Like she'd believe me.' Alan actually liked his ex-wife, more so now they weren't married, but he knew her limitations. Open-mindedness wasn't one of Chrissie's attributes and she'd taken an instant dislike to Sarah Jane the moment they'd met. 'No, I'll say nothing to her. But…'

And it had been what followed that "but" that had so shocked, horrified and above all, dismayed Maria.

'But tomorrow morning, I'm putting this house on the market. What Sarah Jane does is her business and I'm sure the world's a better place for it. But it's not kids' stuff, Maria, it's dangerous. And we're going to have to move.'

Chapter Two

Wall of lies

Across the road, in Sarah Jane Smith's amazing attic, full of alien artefacts, pictures, computers and post-it notes stuck to the walls, Sarah Jane and Luke were looking through a telescope up at the stars in the dusky night sky.

'There,' Sarah Jane said. 'Just below Bellatrix, on Orion's shoulder. Do you see, Luke? That's where they'll appear.'

Before Luke could focus, the attic door was loudly pushed open and Maria stood there, clearly upset.

She ran to Sarah Jane, and hugged her. 'Dad says we're moving. He says I can't have anything to do with you any more. He says it's too dangerous.'

'Well, it is dangerous,' Luke said.

'That's not the point,' Maria shot back.

Sarah Jane eased Maria away from her, smiling. 'But no parent wants to see their child in danger,' she explained. 'I know your father has a lot more to worry about than most dads. You can't blame him for wanting to keep you safe.'

But Maria wasn't going to accept this. 'If you'd talk to him…'

'I don't know what to say.'

Maria was pleading now. 'Tell him about the magic. How wonderful it all is. Tell him all about the amazing wonders of the universe.'

Luke cleared his throat, about to point something out that neither Sarah Jane nor Maria had noticed – that Alan Jackson was stood in the attic doorway, but he never got the chance because Alan spoke first.

'Perhaps it is full of wonders,' he said. 'But as you said about the Slitheen and so on, it's not all sparkling stars and moonlight.'

Maria looked straight at him, taking a deep breath. Clearly determined not to be angry with her dad. 'Yeah, well, sometimes things from space are scary and evil – but how's that different from things on Earth? And sometimes things from space are amazing and beautiful, and you realise how incredible it all is. We're part of something much bigger than living on Bannerman Road. Life is so much more than most people will ever know, and I've been really lucky. I've seen that. And… and I can't just give it up.'

Alan looked to Sarah Jane. 'This is too much to take in.'

'That's the universe, Alan,' Sarah Jane replied. 'Once it's chosen to show you some of its secrets, you can't ever turn your back on it. None of us can.'

Alan thought back to standing in the attic a few days earlier, to seeing Sarah Jane and Maria and Luke and Clyde dealing with the Trickster. And remembering how his fear had been ultimately swept aside by pride. Pride in his amazing daughter and her astonishing friends.

He took a deep breath. 'No. No, I suppose not. I've got a lot to get used to, haven't I?'

And Maria hugged him.

Sarah Jane nodded to Luke, and he indicated to Alan Jackson that he should look through the window next to the telescope.

'The Kalazian Lights are about to appear. The last time they were visible from Earth was four thousand years ago. The universe is smiling at us tonight.'

As Alan joined the others to look up at the dusky

sky, he said quietly so that only Sarah Jane could hear: 'Let's hope it always does.'

It was around teatime, a day after the Kalazian Lights had enthralled them all, Alan Jackson included, that Sarah Jane Smith's world turned upside down.

She wandered into the living room, where Luke was sat, head buried in a book about dinosaurs that tied in nicely with the T-shirt he was wearing, his favourite one with a stegosaurus emblazoned across the front. Sarah Jane had bought him the T-shirt on a day out to the Natural History Museum a couple of months back, and he rarely took it off. The TV was on in the background. Sarah Jane wasn't really listening to the programme Luke was clearly not actually watching, but she got the gist. A couple of parents, eyes red-rimmed with distress were making an appeal for the safe return of a missing child.

'It's been five months since we last saw Ashley,' the woman in the grey top was saying mournfully, her hair tugged back in a tight ponytail. 'But we pray every night that he's out there, somewhere, unharmed. And that he'll come back to us soon.'

Her husband took over, blue shirt, beige jacket.

Sarah Jane noticed things like that slightly more than the actual words.

'If you're out there, watching this,' the dad said, please just call your mum and dad, Ashley. Please.'

The dad hugged his distraught wife, and Sarah Jane's attention was drawn to the distinctive, and rather unattractive scar beneath his left ear.

'If the human race is going to survive global warming, Luke,' Sarah Jane admonished lightly, 'you're going to have to give it a helping hand – not to mention helping with my electricity bill.'

Luke didn't even grunt a response.

Sarah Jane sighed and rummaged on the sofa for the remote, to switch the TV off.

'If you can't have children of your own,' the mum was saying on the screen, 'if that's why you've taken my boy – because you're lonely – how do you think I feel?'

And something in the words made Sarah Jane watch more closely.

The dad took over again, hugging his wife closer to him. 'If anybody knows where Ashley is, please contact the West Ealing police.'

And Sarah Jane's eyes widened as a photo of the missing Ashley Stafford was flashed up.

Under the photo was the mother's voice. 'Whoever's got him, you might think you're caring for him. You might think you love him. But he belongs back with us. His real mum and dad.'

'That's me,' Luke breathed at her shoulder. 'I don't understand.'

Sarah Jane couldn't speak. The picture of this missing Ashley Stafford was indeed Luke Smith.

Her mind raced. But Luke had been created, by the Bane. She'd been there, she'd seen him seconds after he was "activated". Maria had been the first person he'd met, talked to. Born into a strange world, physically aged thirteen, but with the innocence of a child. He'd come on in leaps and bounds in the last six months – his fantastic mind learning and adapting so much, that no one outside his immediate 'family' knew of his origins. To teachers and kids at school, he was just Luke. Hyper-intelligent, slightly socially awkward, Luke Smith.

Only Sarah Jane and her closest friends knew he was actually one hundred percent Bane-created Luke Smith.

Even Mr Smith had confirmed Luke's bewildering origins.

And yet… Sarah Jane had never actually seen him as the Archetype, as the Bane referred to him. She hadn't witnessed that creation.

What if the Bane had stolen Luke, emptied his

mind of his life as Ashley Stafford?

What if Sarah Jane had, however unwittingly, been holding him here instead of looking deeper into his background? Maybe she would have found out the truth.

Maybe she hadn't wanted to – maybe Luke represented the child she'd never had the time in her life to have herself. To bring up, to love and cherish, to -

'But you're my mum,' said Luke, breaking into her thoughts.

Sarah Jane took Luke's hand and squeezed it with a reassurance she didn't really feel qualified to give.

'Come on, I know someone who can give us some answers.' She led the confused Luke upstairs to the attic.

Chapter Three

Hidden danger

'**M**r Smith,' Sarah Jane said, as she and Luke dashed into the room at the very top of the house, 'more than ever, I need you.'

But Mr Smith was already out, as if he'd anticipated Sarah Jane's arrival. And on his screen was a freeze frame of the distraught mother from the news report, staring out at Sarah Jane, accusingly.

'I have been monitoring the news reports,' Mr Smith reported somewhat pointlessly. His serene voice as calm and collected, as always. Whether reporting worldwide disaster or delivering the state of the weather, Mr Smith always spoke with the same manner, which normally Sarah Jane found reassuring and friendly.

But today, a day already less than usual, there was something in his voice that caused a momentary frown on her face. It was as if he was too eager to help. She tried to remember if he'd ever anticipated her needs before, emerged from his chimney stack before, without being asked.

'The first thing I think I should do is scan Luke.'

'Why?' Luke asked.

Sarah Jane squeezed his hand again. 'It's all right. We have to be sure.'

'This won't hurt at all, Luke,' Mr Smith said, and Luke was suddenly scanned by a pencil thin red beam of light, running up and down him from top to bottom. Mr Smith did this, four or five times.

'Well,' asked Sarah Jane when he'd stopped.

The pause seemed interminable and the mood wasn't helped when all Mr Smith said after a minute was that he was assessing the information.

After another minute, the longest, as far as they were concerned, in Sarah Jane and Luke's lives, Mr Smith delivered his verdict.

'My cellular scan and DNA cross-reference with the available medical records of Ashley Stafford are concluded.'

'And?' said Luke after a long wait.

'I have a comprehensive genetic match.'

'Which means?'

'Luke and Ashley Stafford are the same person.'

For Sarah Jane this was the worst possible result. 'There has to be a mistake…'

'I do not make mistakes, Sarah Jane.' Mr Smith sounded almost cross at the suggestion. 'That is a human trait.'

'But the Bane made me,' cried Luke. 'You know they did.'

'The last time Ashley Stafford was seen was getting off the Bubbleshock Factory bus three days before you brought Luke to Bannerman Road,' Mr Smith said.

Sarah Jane threw an arm around her son, as if protecting him not just from the bad news, but from the whole world. 'This doesn't make any sense. Luke was never born. He doesn't have a navel.'

Mr Smith was as matter-of-fact as ever. 'Bane society, being egg-born, find the mammalian navel crude and offensive. It would appear that they surgically removed Ashley's –'

'My name is Luke,' Luke said, quietly.

'My apologies. They surgically removed Luke's navel at the time he was programmed to be their archetype.'

Luke was devastated. He looked at Sarah Jane. 'But you're my mum, not her,' he threw a look at the face on Mr Smith's screen.

Sarah Jane was not going to give up. 'Mr Smith, is there any chance that –' but Mr Smith didn't let her finish.

'Chances of DNA mismatch, approximately four billion to one.'

Sarah Jane held Luke tighter, in case it was the last time she would ever be able to do so.

Across the road at number 36, Maria and Alan Jackson were in similar shock and distress, having seen the news. As they began asking each other unanswerable questions, the front door was opened by an exultant Chrissie.

'I knew there was something not quite right about Contrary Jane and that so-called son of hers.'

Maria was in no mood to chastise her mother's irritating habit of deliberately getting Sarah Jane's name wrong. Instead she just said 'It's a mistake. It has to be.'

'Oh, and why's that?' asked Chrissie.

But Maria couldn't answer. It was just… a feeling, a trust in Sarah Jane and Luke that her mum could never understand. Would never understand. And even if Chrissie knew the truth about Sarah Jane and what they did, she'd still choose not to believe in Sarah Jane. Chrissie was like that. Maria loved her mum dearly, but she could also be very annoying when she put her mind to it. And Sarah Jane was a sore point with Chrissie for reasons Maria had never really got to the bottom of.

'Exactly,' Chrissie said triumphantly. 'So we'll let the police make up their minds about that, shall we?'

Alan was aghast. 'The police? You didn't call the police?'

But Chrissie was unrepentant. 'I've told you time and time again, there's something wrong with that woman. I can smell it on her.'

She flicked the front room curtain back, to reveal to the others a police car pulling up outside number 13.

'Told you. She's a weirdo. You see.'

Moments later, Sarah Jane and Luke were stood in her hallway, a policeman holding the front door open, expectantly.

'What's going to happen to us?' Luke fretted.

Sarah Jane tried to sound calm and casual, as if

this happened every day, but wasn't hiding her real emotions very well at all.

'I expect the police will take us to the station. They'll question me, and PC Ford here will take you to see your parents again. Your real parents.'

She tried to smile for Luke's benefit, but only just managed a quick grimace.

'So why can't I remember them,' he replied. 'I know all sorts of things – quantum theory, Colluphid's Law of Hyper-Dimensional Mechanics, I can spot the flaws in Einstein's theory of relativity too – I can remember every page of every book I've ever read… so why can't I remember them?'

Sarah Jane took Luke by the shoulders and looked him straight in the eye.

'I wish I had all the answers. I know this is difficult, you must know I do.'

Luke nodded and Sarah Jane took a deep breath before carrying on. 'But this isn't a bad day. Mr and Mrs Stafford are your real parents. They love you.'

And Luke's forehead creased into a frown of confusion.

'Don't you love me?'

And if ever a question could break Sarah Jane's heart, it was that one. But she had to go on, for Luke's sake; to try and lessen the pain for both of them.

'Of course I do,' she said. 'But you don't belong with me. Your parents have spent months looking for you. The Bane took you away from them, and broke their hearts. Today is the most wonderful day in their lives because they get you back. And you are going to be an ordinary human boy again, with parents that care for you, and won't let anything bad happen to you. They'll protect you in a way I never could.'

She tried not to let the tears she could feel welling up, show in her eyes. It wouldn't be right or fair on Luke. She had to be so strong for both of them.

'And so this is the best day of your life too,' she finished up. 'You'll see.'

The waiting PC Ford eased Luke away from her, and Sarah Jane's hands fell uselessly to her sides as Luke was marched through the front door, out of 13 Bannerman Road and her life for good.

Out in the street, by the corner where Bannerman Road met Old Forest Road, quite a crowd had gathered, mainly neighbours who had got to know Luke and his odd mum by sight over the last few months, most of whom had seen the news reports and were responding with a mixture of confusion, disgust, sorrow or disbelief. Amongst them were the Jacksons, Alan feeling sad for Sarah Jane, Maria determined to protect Luke and Chrissie smug that she had been responsible for bringing this to a head.

'Here she comes,' she sniggered. 'Calamity Jane.'

'Oh drop it Chrissie,' Alan snapped. 'You've got your victory, now be quiet, for Maria's sake if nothing else.'

Maria swung round on her mum. 'This is all your fault.'

Chrissie was appalled. 'Hey, I don't go around kidnapping young boys and passing them off as my own.'

Alan led her back towards his home. 'For goodness sake, that's enough.'

'You watch,' Chrissie was saying as Alan all but threw her back into the house. 'Once this gets to court it'll all come out. Goodness knows what else she's hiding…' But Chrissie Jackson's guesses were cut off as Alan slammed the front door shut.

Maria watched them go as a policeman led Luke down the driveway and onto the streets. 'Don't be nervous, lad,' he was saying. 'Soon get you back to your parents.'

Luke twisted his arm away, and looked back to where Sarah Jane was being eased along behind, a WPC holding her arm firmly.

Then a woman's voice rang out. 'Ashley? Ashley!!'

And the woman from the TV was there, pushing through the crowd.

'Oh Ashley, thank God,' she cried. 'Thank God you're all right. Oh my baby! My beautiful baby boy!'

Luke just stared at her. As if he'd never seen her before in his life. 'Are you really my mother? Was I born from your womb?'

The odd phrasing of the question clearly threw the woman who claimed to be his real mother. 'Ashley, what are you…?'

And then a man was at her shoulder. 'It's all right, love,' he said to his wife. 'Hello, son. Of course she's your mum. Don't you remember us? Son?'

Luke just shrugged and spoke the truth as he knew it. 'No. Not at all.'

There was a moment's silence before Mrs Stafford shrieked with a rage that only an angry mother could, and ran towards Sarah Jane, who had to be protected by the WPC and another officer. 'What have you done to him, you witch?'

PC Ford, the policeman who'd been in the house, stepped before Mrs Stafford, holding her back. 'Mrs Stafford, please,' he started, but the distraught mother tried to strike at Sarah Jane.

'I haven't hurt him,' Sarah Jane protested. 'I swear to you, Luke – Ashley, he had an accident. He's lost his memory. I had no idea he even had parents looking for him.'

And Mr Stafford was there now, comforting his angry wife, calming her down. 'What, you thought the fairies had left him under a mulberry bush, did you? You make me sick!'

And Sarah Jane could say nothing, because Mr Stafford was right. She never even considered the option that Luke hadn't been created by the Bane. Not once. She just took it for granted and when Mr Smith had created the adoption papers, she'd never asked him to do any checks, just in case. Although surely, Mr Smith would've done that automatically, so why didn't any of this show up?

Before she could ponder this further, the WPC whispered in her ear that they ought to get going to the station, for Sarah Jane's safety more than anything else. With a nod, Sarah Jane Smith let herself be led away.

As she was going towards the police car, Sarah Jane caught a last look at Luke, being placed into the back seat of the Stafford's car by the father.

'Mum!' he shouted to her, but Mr Stafford slammed the door shut, cutting off the sound of his voice. 'Come on you,' he said, harshly. 'Time we got you home.'

'Darling,' added Mrs Stafford, almost as an afterthought.

Clyde Langer felt utterly useless. Maria had just texted him to tell him the gist of what was going on, and that she'd fill him in on the rest later.

His best mate. Ever. Taken away by strangers. And Sarah Jane treated like some sort of criminal.

'Oh this is so not happening,' he said out loud.

'What's that, sweetheart?' asked Carla, Clyde's mum, as she carried more books into the library stockroom.

Clyde had offered to help him mum this evening. The library where she worked was doing a stock take over the weekend, trying to work out which books, CDs and DVDs had been borrowed by the great and good of Ealing and never returned.

Or had been misfiled.

Or had generally gone astray. Twice a year the library did this, and twice a year Clyde helped out. He liked doing it – he adored his mum (not that he was uncool enough to let people at school know this – he had an image to keep up, you know) and since his dad had gone, they spent as much time together as they could. And Carla was the best mum ever, but she'd never understand about Sarah Jane and aliens and stuff. Clyde hated keeping secrets from her, but knew it was for the best.

But Carla and Sarah Jane knew one another, and they'd become quite friendly over the last few months, mainly because they both were into books, which Clyde could never quite get his head around.

Carla was always inviting Sarah Jane round for tea and coffee and although Sarah Jane wormed her way out of it each time, it wasn't through any dislike of Carla, but due to Sarah Jane's general discomfort around other adults.

So when Clyde explained what was going on, Carla was immediately sympathetic. 'Listen darling, I love the fact that you're giving up your Sunday to be here with me, but you and Luke… well, I understand how important he is to you. You go and see if you can help. Just try and be back for food tonight, okay?'

'You're the best, mum,' Clyde said, kissing her cheek. 'Laters!'

And he was off, almost running across town, then the park, to get towards Maria's house.

Chapter Four

A change of identity

Chief Inspector Robert Lines sighed at the woman in front of him, as he sat down at the table. He turned off his mobile phone and placed in front of them both a fax he'd been called out to get.

The fax was from a Government department, C19, and was a Level Four Clearance form from the Unified Intelligence Task force. Sarah Jane didn't even smile as Lines tapped at the UNIT logo with his pen.

'You have powerful friends, it seems, Miss Smith.'

'My friends have nothing to do with it. I've

done nothing wrong.' Sarah Jane eased a mug of untouched cold tea away from her.

Lines pulled a photocopied sheet from a buff file on the table as he took a swig from his own mug. It was a copy of the Adoption Agency form that, unknown to Lines, Mr Smith had created and secreted amongst other such forms, to give the impression that Sarah Jane had adopted Luke legally, some months earlier.

Lines then looked at more papers. 'You were brought up by your Aunt, I see.'

Sarah Jane nodded. 'My parents died when I was a baby.'

'I can see why adopting kids is important to you. Your Aunt also had a ward she looked after.'

Sarah Jane sighed. 'Yes, after I had left home.'

Lines nodded. 'Brendan Richards, now working for a software development company in Silicon Valley, I see.' He smiled at Sarah Jane. 'Brainy kids you Smith's take under your wing. Ashley, or Luke, also very bright, according to his school reports from Park Vale. A pattern, you might say.'

'And from the school the Stafford's sent him to?'

The policeman shrugged. 'Not requested those, Miss Smith. The Stafford's aren't being investigated.' He tapped the UNIT file again. 'I don't know whether you are lucky or I'm getting brushed off with a cover-up. Either way, you're free to go.'

'Thank you.' Sarah Jane stood up and picked up her coat. 'And thank you for the tea. It was very nice. Probably.'

'Stay away from Ashley Stafford, Miss Smith,' Lines offered. 'Because your contacts won't be able to help you every time.'

With a terse smile, Sarah Jane walked out of the room.

26 Chalsey Grove, Luke realised, was going to be his new home. It was a simple end-of -terrace house in Hammersmith, with a nice brick wall, a nice wrought iron gate, leading to a nice terracotta pathway that led to a nice wooden front door. Inside, there was a nice hall, leading to a nice living room, a nice kitchen and a nice downstairs lavatory.

Luke felt sick as he looked around. The place was clean and neat and tidy. The walls were painted with neutral colours or adorned with plain wallpaper. A couple of paintings were hung on the walls, but they were bland watercolours of woods and grasslands.

There were no photographs by the phone, no knick-knacks on the mantelpiece, no soul.

'What do you think, son?' asked Mr Stafford.

'Home sweet home,' Mrs Stafford laughed, throwing a triumphant look at her husband.

Mr Stafford led Luke through to the kitchen. On the side were six identical mugs. And six plates. And six bowls, all identically patterned.

It was a nice kitchen with nice things in it.

'It's… nice,' was all Luke could say, frowning at the mugs, looking so perfectly clean and unchipped.

Luke longed for the chaos of Sarah Jane's house. He'd never thought about it before, about how there, nothing really matched, but everything had a story behind it. Mugs that were gifts, marks on the walls that were accidents, cracks in the stained glass window that were the result of age.

26 Chalsey Grove had none of that. No life, no history. No sense that a loving family had lived here.

And again, his "parents" were exchanging looks he couldn't understand, as if they were expecting him to react in a certain way rather than just do what he felt was natural, which was not to trust them one little bit.

'We've got footie club on Thursday night,' Mr Stafford said encouragingly.

Luke would've laughed if it wasn't so scary.

Him? Football? If all this was true, if the Bane creating him was a lie, if his whole life with Sarah Jane Smith was a result of him losing his memory, surely he couldn't be totally the opposite to Ashley Stafford? But football? Luke could work out the exact speed and point to kick a football, to get it onto the trajectory needed to get past players and goalkeeper, sure. But actually kick the ball and not fall flat on his face? Never…

'Football?'

'Yeah. You and me, and the lads from the youth club. Pizza and coke afterwards.' Mr Stafford seemed genuinely confused. 'You remember that don't you?'

Luke shook his head. 'I don't like football.'

'What did that woman do to you?' Mrs Stafford breathed. 'What did she do to my baby boy?'

She opened a cupboard in the kitchen. 'Why don't I sort out some food before bed? It's been a long day for you.'

Luke shrugged. 'Can I go and lie down. Please?'

'So formal,' Mr Stafford laughed. 'Course you can, son. You remember the way?'

But Luke shook his head. 'I don't remember this house at all.'

Mr Stafford led him up the stairs. Three bedrooms

and a bathroom. One of which had a sign on it.

ASHLEY'S ROOM – PARENTS KEEP OUT UNLESS INVITED

'Am I allowed in, son?' Mr Stafford said in a tone that suggested this was an old routine for them both. And Luke felt a pang off sorrow for both of these strange new people because if he really was Ashley Stafford, his lack of memory had to be as awful for them as it was confusing for him.

'Yeah,' he said. 'Come in,' hoping that was the right tone of voice. Friendly. Like Clyde would do it.

Clyde. His best friend. Clyde, who was miles away.

They went in and Luke got the biggest shock so far. If the rest of the house was more ordered than a show house in a new housing estate, his room was chaos on a colossal scale.

The wall was almost invisible behind posters of footballers, and pop groups - UNIT 4, and a girl duo, In-Demand.

On the bedside table was a photo of him. Of Ashley anyway, in an Everton football strip, balancing the ball expertly on his knee, a huge grin on his face.

On shelves were model aeroplanes, a blue kite

and even a model of a big demon-thing from a movie Luke knew he'd not seen, because he recalled Clyde pointing out how uncool he was for never having done so.

He turned to speak to Mr Stafford, but he just pointed to the bed. 'Have a rest, I'll call you when your mum's sorted food.'

Mum.

How would he get used to calling that woman downstairs "mum" without Sarah Jane's face coming into his mind's eye?

By the time he'd thought that thought, the door was closed.

And audibly locked.

Okay, that was, as Maria would say, dead weird.

He looked at the unfamiliar room, full of unfamiliar things and sat on the unfamiliar bed and wondered if he'd ever like this new life. Old life. Whatever it was.

And for the first time ever that he could remember, he felt utterly and completely alone.

Downstairs, Mr Stafford plonked himself down on the sofa next to his wife with a grin.

'Ready?' she asked.

He nodded.

She turned on the TV with the remote but instead of a picture, a series of swirling, gyrating patterns of light appeared.

'Xylok,' she said, 'are you there? We've got the boy!'

And from the TV came a strange electronic burble that could have been laughter. Indeed, it probably was, because Mr and Mrs Stafford joined in, laughing at some huge joke that only they understood.

They and the Xylok.

Chapter Five

Conspiracy

It was about nine o'clock that night by the time Sarah Jane Smith had got back to Bannerman Road. The media circus had vanished from outside her home.

Home.

It didn't feel like home any more. It was just a house. A big, empty house. Just as it had been before Luke came to live there.

She'd coped quite well without a son before, she'd adjust again. Throw herself back into work.

It'd be fine.

She looked up the stairs, past the framed newspaper cuttings and magazine covers that signified her career in journalism. There, up at the top, was a photograph that Luke had asked to put up there. Luke, Maria, Clyde and Sarah Jane at a skateboard park. Alan Jackson had taken it not long ago.

Her family. That's how she'd come to think of them.

'Sarah Jane?'

Sarah Jane didn't turn to look at Maria. She couldn't. She had to focus. Move on. No more kids in her life. And that included Maria Jackson.

'Luke has gone,' she said, facing the wall, staring at a spot below the photo. 'Back to his real parents. Back where he belongs. Mr Smith confirmed it. The Bane kidnapped Ashley Stafford, did things to him. I got it wrong. Not for the first time.'

'I'm really sorry,' Maria said quietly.

'No,' Sarah Jane said, taking a deep breath. She still wouldn't face Maria. 'No, it's for the best. I'm not cut out to be a parent. Children have no place in my life. I told you, when we first met, my life is dangerous.'

'You don't mean that.'

And Sarah Jane finally turned to face her, but kept any warmth or emotion out of her voice. She had to. It was important that Maria understood.

'I can't afford to be worrying about other people, they're a distraction. These last few months, I've been lucky. I can't expect that to hold up for ever.

So you go home, go tell your father he's right. You should put the house on the market and he and you and Clyde too, you should forget all about me and everything you've seen.'

Maria just looked at her. 'Oh yeah? And how are we going to do that?' she asked, not unreasonably. 'What happened to never turning your back on the universe?'

Sarah Jane closed her eyes for a second before looking Maria straight in the eye. 'Sometimes you have to. Sometimes it's the only way to survive.'

Maria just stared at her, then turned on her heel and left.

And Sarah Jane let out a deep, pained sigh. She glanced up the stairs again, her eyes settling on the photo at the skateboard park.

Then she headed upstairs, past the photo and further up, into her attic.

If Sarah Jane was surprised to see that Mr Smith was already out, she didn't comment on it, choosing to flop down instead on the red chaise longue that occupied one end of the room.

'If I may, Sarah Jane…' Mr Smith began.

'I didn't call you,' she snapped.

Unfazed by her abrupt response, Mr Smith merely continued in his smooth as silk tones. 'Perhaps you

Chrissie tells Alan and Maria that she has called the police about Sarah Jane and Luke.

Sarah Jane tries to remain calm when the police come for Luke.

Sarah Jane anxiously watches as Luke is reunited with his 'real' parents.

The Police lead Sarah Jane away to question her about Luke.

Luke doesn't want to go with the Staffords, whom he has never met before.

Nathan Goss at work in the Pharos Institute.

Sarah Jane is fascinated by Nathan Goss' research project.

Mr and Mrs Stafford are not who they claim to be.

The MITRE project headset is kept locked in a cabinet.

20-80

The hunt is on! Luke escapes from the lab as the child Slitheen gives chase.

Sarah Jane, Maria and Alan confront the family Slitheen at the Institute.

Korst Gogg Thek, the child Slitheen, grabs hold of Maria by the neck.

The family Slitheen realise that they have been used by Mr Smith, as well.

Alan, Maria, Sarah Jane and the Slitheen watch as the moon moves closer to Earth.

didn't realise that you need me.'

'Yeah, well, not tonight I don't.'

'You need a purpose,' he continued, relentlessly. 'All things in the universe need a purpose. Without purpose, we cease to be.'

Sarah Jane frowned. That was getting a bit philosophical for a Sunday night. 'What are you talking about?'

'I've been monitoring experiments at the Pharos Institute. They are exploring the possibilities of para-science. Carrying out tests in telekinetic energy.'

Sarah Jane considered this. Way back, when working for Metropolitan Magazine, she'd been sent on an assignment to cover it's launch. It was ostensibly set up to study paranormal phenomena, but with very little success.

'They have recently seemingly perfected a way to harness telekinetic energy. The ability to move objects with just the power of one's mind.'

'I know what it means, Mr Smith,' Sarah Jane said a bit waspishly. 'Why are you telling me this?'

'I believe they are cheating. They are using alien technology.'

Sarah Jane's interest was now piqued. 'Well, perhaps I should pay them a visit tomorrow. And this time,' she added, almost to herself, 'I won't have any children to slow me down.'

'Indeed,' Mr Smith agreed. 'No children.'

And if Sarah Jane had been listening more closely to Mr Smith's tone, she might have detected a level of satisfaction in those last two words more than a computer ought to have expressed.

It was Monday morning and Luke wanted to go to school. But he hadn't any of his own clothes with him and clearly his new/old parents didn't have a white shirt or Park Vale School tie in his wardrobe. He ran his hands over an orange hooded sweatshirt that he couldn't imagine ever wearing. It reminded him of the orange jumpsuits he'd seen American prisoners wear on TV. And that's how he felt this morning – a prisoner. He tried the door handle again but it was still locked from last night, after dinner. He'd asked Mr Stafford why the door had been locked, but all he got was a comment about him not running away again. When Luke reacted to this by asking if he'd run away before, his "parents" had given each other an odd look and said it was a precaution, for his own safety. 'We're just being over-cautious, love,' Mrs Stafford had said.

He could hear voices downstairs now, presumably Mr Stafford getting ready for work doing… whatever it was he did.

He pressed his head closer to the door, but couldn't hear anything else. They'd stopped talking. Perhaps Mr Stafford had left, so why wasn't he being let out?

Then he jumped, as suddenly the sound of the lock outside being turned echoed through his head and he barely got across to the window, trying to look innocent, before Mrs Stafford came in.

'Where's my school uniform?' Luke asked her.

Mrs Stafford shrugged. 'You don't go to school. Not today at least.'

'But I want to see my friends…'

Mrs Stafford just laughed. 'Oh right. Clyde Langer. Maria Jackson. Jacob West. Dave Finn – that lot?'

And Luke thought that was… odd. 'How do you know all their names?'

Mrs Stafford just shrugged. 'Who cares. You won't see them again.' And she slammed and locked the door again.

Luke put on the orange hoodie. If he was to remain a prisoner, he might as well look the part.

A few hours later, it was lunchtime at Park Vale School, but Maria and Clyde hadn't got much of an appetite.

'So that's it? No more monsters? No more saving the world?' Clyde was incredulous when Maria told him about her conversation with Sarah Jane from the night before.

'She's devastated about Luke,' explained Maria.

'Yeah, she's not the only one,' Clyde said, glancing at the empty seat next to him where he best mate usually sat. 'So where have they taken him?'

'Hammersmith, apparently. I suppose Ashley will go back to his old school.'

'Luke,' Clyde corrected her automatically. 'There's no such person as Ashley Stafford, I'm sure of it.'

'How?'

Clyde just shrugged. 'I just know it.' He slapped the table top angrily. 'Damn, and I've just got him into Kasabian. It was onto the Arctic Monkeys next – and then after another few weeks, I could've had him passing as cool.'

Maria laughed. 'Then that wouldn't be Luke either.'

Clyde grinned. 'Yeah, but it's worth a try.'

Maria sighed. 'But if, just saying, he is really Ashley, then the Bane must've really messed him about.'

Clyde nodded. 'I bet finding out he'd got a real

dad and mum messed him up more.'

'I hope he's all right,' said Maria.

And Clyde stood up, stuffing the last of his sandwich in is mouth. 'Why don't we find out, yeah? If they live in Hammersmith, it's not a long journey from here. Have you got the address?'

Maria shrugged. 'It was in the paper I think.'

'Then come on,' Clyde said, gathering his stuff together.

Maria looked around at the other kids in the hall, and the teachers. 'Bell's going any minute. Lessons. We'll never get out.'

'Look,' said Clyde. 'If our days of fighting aliens are really over, sneaking off lessons once in a while is gonna be all the excitement we're going to get.'

Maria smiled grabbed her bag and the two of them headed out.

They'd got as far as crossing the playground when the bell went. And as far as the teachers' car park, hiding behind Mrs Pittman's car, when Maria made the first dash for the gates.

A voice rang out, causing Clyde to stay put, out of sight.

It was their class teacher, Mr Cunningham. 'Maria Jackson,' he yelled. 'Where exactly do you think you're going?'

'To the library, sir,' Maria said, lamely.

'I think you're due in Mr Cairn's double French, actually,' he said.

Clyde watched as Maria's shoulders sagged as she made her way back towards the main building.

When she, and Mr Cunningham, were well out of sight, Clyde was up and out.

Park Vale station was just around the corner and from there it was a short ride to Ealing Broadway. A couple of tube rides later, and he was in Hammersmith, standing at the end of Chalsey Grove, looking for number 26.

There it was.

He rang the doorbell and after a few seconds, it opened. To reveal Mrs Stafford, he presumed. 'Hi. I'm a mate of Lu - Ashley's. Is he in?'

'No. He's at school.'

But Clyde stood his ground, his best grin on his face. 'You know, you don't look much like him, do you?'

'Well, he takes after his dad, doesn't he?' Mrs Stafford frowned, and her mouth curled into a smile. 'You trying to say he's not our Ashley? Oh, I get it. That Sarah Jane Smith sent you, right?'

Before Clyde could confirm or deny this, Mrs Stafford grabbed a photograph in a frame from out of a set of drawers nearby. Odd place to keep a photo, Clyde reckoned.

It showed Luke/Ashley with Mr and Mrs Stafford. Luke/Ashley was clutching a skateboard, grinning broadly. 'His last birthday,' she said by way of explanation. 'We gave him that skateboard.'

'Good was he? On the skateboard I mean?' asked Clyde as casually as he could manage.

'Course he was. He's our Ashley. Good at everything he is.' She passed him the photo. 'So you take that back to your Sarah Jane Smith and you tell her my boy is back where he belongs!'

And the door was slammed shut in Clyde's face. But he didn't mind, he was grinning now.

As he walked down the street, he failed to look up. If he had, he'd have seen Luke, locked in his bedroom, hammering on the window, calling Clyde's name.

Clyde reached the end of the street but instead of heading back to the tube, he wandered into a park, where some boys were practising basketball, and a couple of old people were walking their dogs.

He called Maria on his mobile.

After a few rings, she answered, hushed. 'Had to say I needed a toilet break,' she explained, 'so I don't have long.'

'Right. Well, this whole Luke thing is suss. His so-called mum wouldn't let me see him and you know what she said they gave him on his last birthday? A skateboard. You've seen him on a skateboard. No sense of balance at all.'

Maria laughed. Luke did indeed spend more time falling off skateboards than anything else. But, she suggested, that could be an after-effect of what the Bane had done to him.

'I don't care what the Bane did or didn't do – you don't loose skills like that. It's instinct. And my instinct says that this photo they've given me is suss, too.'

'How?'

'Photos can be faked. I'm gonna show it to Sarah Jane and see what she has to say.'

Chapter Six

The powerful enemy

S ome miles out of London, Sarah Jane Smith was standing in the reception area of a hi-tech establishment, established, so the plaque on the wall stated "for the furthering of paranormal research and investigation". And imprinted on every door and glass wall (of which there were more than a few), was the legend A BEACON OF POSSIBILITY, above an engraving of a customised atomic energy symbol, but geared more to the Pharos Institute's directive of exploring the mind.

Sarah Jane smiled at the receptionist. 'Hello, I

just wondered how much longer –' but she got no further because a door opened and a tall, elegant woman walked over, hand held out ready to shake, which Sarah Jane did automatically.

'Miss Smith, I am so sorry for keeping you waiting, it's terribly rude of me. How was your trip? Have you had a cup of tea, yet?'

'Oh, fine and I don't need a drink, thank you,' Sarah Jane responded.

'Marvellous,' the woman replied. 'My name is Rivers. I'm in charge of this place.'

'Professor Celeste Rivers?'

'You've heard of me? You are either a very good journalist, Miss Smith, or a mad stalker. I do hope it's the former.'

And Sarah Jane relaxed. She liked this woman with the easy manner and genuine smile that wasn't just on her lips but was in her eyes as well.

Professor Rivers led her down a corridor. 'If I recall from my briefing notes, you were one of the journalists here the day the Institute opened, yes?'

Sarah Jane nodded. 'That's right.' She looked up at an impressive selection of photographs of top people connected with the Institute's work over the years.

'Without the pioneering work of people like

these,' Professor Rivers said, 'we'd still be floundering in the dark.'

Sarah Jane recognised a lot of the people from her past researches – Peter Fairley, Patricia Conway, Ann Reynolds, Bryan Cawston…

'I'm impressed,' she said.

Professor Rivers gestured around them as they passed room after room of activity involving white coated scientists and researchers. 'I'm glad. We don't have nearly enough media interest. Most people still write off our work as that of cranks, but we're in good company. Galileo and Copernicus were both dismissed by their blinkered scientific contemporaries.'

Professor Rivers opened a door, and indicated for Sarah Jane to lead the way in.

'Of course,' Sarah Jane said as she passed into the room, 'Galileo and Copernicus weren't carrying out experiments into the paranormal.'

Professor Rivers held up a hand, and smiled. 'Ah, but don't forget, Sir Isaac Newton and Thomas Edison both had strong personal interests in the "paranormal", Miss Smith.'

'It's your work into telekinesis that I'm particularly curious about.'

The Professor grinned wider. 'Then, Miss Smith,

you are in for a treat.' She waved her arm around. 'This is our telekinesis laboratory.' She pressed a button on a wall and a screen slid up, revealing another room beyond. 'Two-way mirror,' she explained. We see in, they can't see us.'

A technician was sat a desk, a wire from each temple going into a monitor, and a diadem around his head had more wires leading off it, into a black box.

He was staring at a ball on the floor. He then closed his eyes and the ball started to rise up of its own accord. Jerkily, but it was moving.

'That is... astonishing,' Sarah Jane said, mouth open. She was indeed impressed. Then the ball exploded with a pop, and the technician opened his eyes and sighed loudly.

'Unfortunately we're having a little difficulty with our energy-focus stabilisation. He was using a prototype of MITRE.'

'Which is?'

The professor was in her element now, delighted to be able to talk about the Pharos Institute's work to someone open-minded. 'Magnified Intensification of Telekinetic Reactive Energies. That headset takes the latent raw psychic ability all of us possess and enables the wearer to move the objects with the power of thought.'

'Amazing. And you developed that here?'

'Yes. Our resident child prodigy, Nathan Goss.' She pointed to a side door. 'In here.'

She led Sarah Jane through into a much bigger room, which had a huge LAB 2 painted on one wall. Opposite this wall was another wall with a massive transparent board on it, onto which a young boy was writing furiously.

He kept his back to them, rudely.

Professor Rivers cleared her throat. 'Excuse me, Nathan, but this is Miss Smith. She's here to do a feature about the Institute.'

'So?' was the surly response, as Nathan carried on writing.

'Hello, Nathan,' said Sarah Jane. 'I'm pleased to meet you.'

'I'm working,' snarled Nathan.

'Oh I'm sorry,' she replied. 'To disturb you, I mean. That looks very complex.'

And with a sigh, he finally turned to face the two women.

Sarah Jane thought in some respects he was an attractive lad. Mousy, unkempt hair, looked like he played sports (unusual in a science student, she thought, but good too). But there was something…

not quite right. The down-turned, angry mouth and the blue eyes that glared with something close to hatred at her. She took an involuntary step back.

'Don't waste your time, or mine, asking me to explain,' he shot back, venomously.

Professor Rivers tried to break the tension. 'Miss Smith wants to talk to you about MITRE.'

And Nathan Goss exploded in anger. 'You told her? About MITRE? How stupid can you get?'

'But your work…' Professor Rivers stammered. 'It's important. It needs recognition – and funding. So I thought…'

'You thought? You thought? The day you think will be the day man learns to teleport himself to Mars!'

Professor Rivers put her glasses on, perhaps in an attempt to look more in charge. 'Now, I'm sorry Nathan but that behaviour –'

'Just get out,' Nathan all but screamed, staring straight at Sarah Jane, those angry eyes glaring in a passionate hatred Sarah Jane couldn't understand. She'd never even met this boy before.

'Come along, Miss Smith.' The professor chivvied her out, all apologies and embarrassed pleasantries.

As they reached the door, Sarah Jane swung back

to Nathan Goss.

'I used to know someone your age who could wipe the floor with your intelligence. And you know what? He could wipe the floor with you, too.'

And she was gone.

And the dark, twisted face of Nathan Goss suddenly brightened into a knowing smile as he enjoyed the solitude. 'We'll see about that, Sarah Jane Smith.'

When Sarah Jane got home she went straight up to see Mr Smith in the attic.

She plonked down some of the brochures the apologetic Professor Rivers had given her and told the computer about the events of the morning.

'Nathan Goss is a genius,' he told her. 'He has an IQ of 195, was reading quantum physics at the age of eight. He has already turned down offers from Cambridge, Oxford, Durham and even the Rattigan Academy. Some call him the young Einstein. Others say his potential exceeds Einstein.'

'He's an obnoxious brat,' was Sarah Jane's considered response. 'But there was something about him, Mr Smith. Something in those eyes that made my blood run cold.'

Mr Smith continued as if Sarah Jane hadn't

spoken. 'However, despite his IQ, a telekinetic energiser such as MITRE is still beyond his genius.'

'It could be a terrible weapon.'

'Yes, a destroyer of worlds. In the right hands, with the right mind.'

Sarah Jane was lost in her own thoughts, too distracted to take in what Mr Smith had said. 'Where did it come from then, if he didn't create it?'

'If I could analyse it's composition,' he said encouragingly, 'I could perhaps define its technological origins.'

Sarah Jane half-laughed. 'You mean, sneak back into Pharos and nick one of those headsets?'

'I mean exactly that, Sarah Jane,' the computer responded. 'It would be of great assistance.'

Chapter Seven

Journey into terror

At 26 Chalsey Grove, Luke was trying to get out of his locked room. He was using some of the things he had found in a geometry set in a drawer in the bedside table – a ruler, a triangle and a compass.

He heard the lock finally click back after half an hour's work, just as the doorbell rang.

Was it Clyde, come back for a second attempt? Mrs Stafford opened the door and he could hear a new voice. A kid.

'We have a problem,' the boy was saying.

'What sort of problem?' That was Mr Stafford. So, he hadn't gone to work at all. Something strange was definitely happening here.

'That stupid Rivers woman gave a demonstration of the telekinetic energiser.'

'Who to?' That was Mrs Stafford.

'Oh three guesses.'

'Sarah Jane Smith,' Mr Stafford replied, and Luke's heart leapt at the mention of his mum. His real mum. He knew that now. Whoever the Staffords were, they certainly weren't his biological parents. 'But that doesn't change anything, does it? She can't know anything.'

The boy was furious, speaking to the grown-ups in a way that even Luke thought was downright rude.

'She must know something, you gravy-brained moron, or she wouldn't have been at the Pharos Institute would she?'

Mrs Stafford spoke quietly. 'Okay, but there's no need to talk to us like that –'

But the boy cut her off. 'This is my mission. I shall talk to you any way I choose.'

Luke managed to silently ease the door open and head for the stairs, keeping an eye out for the Stafford's and the boy downstairs, who all seemed to have gone into the living room.

The front door was fifteen steps down, and two

feet across. Freedom.

'The Xylok said she might poke her nose in. It said it would take care of her.' Mrs Stafford sounded alarmed.

The boy responded angrily. 'Oh, I am so sick of hearing "the Xylok says this" and "the Xylok thinks that". The Xylok is just hired help, okay?'

Mr Stafford sighed. 'The plan's too far advanced. Sarah Jane Smith can't stop us. We've got the Bane archetype now.'

And on the stairs, Luke's heart leaped into his mouth – they knew about the Bane. It had all been a set-up.

And he trod on the next step down.

Which gave out a creak that in that moment of silence might just as well have been a gunshot.

Luke didn't wait then, no pretence was necessary, he had to get through the door and out.

He never made it to the bottom stair before Mr Stafford had him pinned down, a cruel armlock causing Luke to yell in pain.

He dragged Luke into the living room, where Mrs Stafford and a boy about his own age, who Luke had never set eyes on before, stood.

Or had he? There was something about the boy's eyes, some powerful feeling of hatred towards Luke coming from them.

Mr Stafford threw Luke onto the sofa. And smiled. 'These new slim-line compression units might handle the gas exchanges better, but they're a bit on the snug side.' And he raised his hand to his forehead.

Luke knew exactly what was going to happen next.

A blast of harsh blue light poured out from Mr Stafford's forehead as he tugged at an invisible zipper.

Mrs Stafford started to do the same.

'Slitheen,' Luke said quietly. 'But you're so slim!'

Mrs Stafford laughed as her Slitheen head popped out from the neck of the human skin she was wearing. 'Amazing isn't it. With all this new technology "borrowed" from the Blathereen back home, I can eat all I want and still be a size eight.'

Luke looked at the boy, already guessing the answer to his next question. He'd known it as soon as he saw the eyes. 'And you?' he said anyway.

Nathan giggled unkindly. 'I'm sure you remember me, Luke Smith,' he said, unzipping his head. 'I'm sure you remember killing my family and leaving me locked in a sealed room to die along with them.'

But the Slitheen boy Luke remembered from a

few months back, when the Slitheen had used his school as a base from which to turn the sun off, had been an overweight, dark-haired lad called Carl.

'Same Slitheen, different skin. I teleported out and survived. My father wasn't so fortunate. And now I will have my revenge!'

Clyde reached the corner of Bannerman Road in time to see Sarah Jane's car roaring out of the drive.

He sighed and was about to head home when he thought about Mr Smith. He'd know if the photo was a fake.

Clyde looked furtively around as he wandered up the drive, knelt down and lifted a plant pot by the front porch.

Sure enough, a spare key, as always.

He let himself into the house and went up the stairs to the attic.

He'd been inside dozens of times, but rarely by himself and he felt a bit guilty about being there without Sarah Jane's say-so.

But this was about Luke, his best mate in the whole world.

'Mr Smith, I need you,' he said.

And with a surge of steam and hydraulics, the computer emerged from the chimney, the gyrating pattern on his screen pulsating slightly faster than normal.

Almost like he was excited, Clyde thought. Then remembered why he was there.

'Mr Smith…'

'Clyde,' the computer interrupted in a way he'd never done before 'What a pleasure.'

'Really? Oh… umm… cool.'

'You have something for me?'

Clyde frowned. 'Yeah. Yeah, how'd you know that? Anyway, look, it's this photo. Of Luke and that pair that reckon they're his mum and dad. See? I think it's a fake. Luke's head stuck onto someone else's body.' He went to place the photo on Mr Smith's little diagnosis drawer. 'I thought you could do your analysing thing and –'

Once again, Mr Smith interrupted him. 'You're right, Clyde. This is a fake. I faked it.'

And Clyde let this sink in. 'Am I missing something?'

'More than you could ever imagine,' Mr Smith replied, icily. 'You see, I am a Xylok. I have a purpose here on Earth. And you, Clyde Langer, are a big part of it.'

And before Clyde could blink, a red beam of pencil thin light blasted out from Mr Smith's control panel and hit Clyde straight in the chest.

And without a sound, Clyde simply vanished.

There was a second or two of silence, and then laughter began echoing around the empty attic.

Mr Smith was laughing. A cold, heartless laugh of dark pleasure…

Chapter Eight

The ordeal

It was dark now. A full moon offered little pockets of brightness through the trees, giving the whole area an other-worldly beauty.

But Sarah Jane Smith had little time to take in the wonders of nature. She was in the grounds of the Pharos Institute, about to commit a criminal act.

Breaking. Entering. Theft.

She had spent so much time teaching Luke about right and wrong and here she was, doing exactly the opposite of what she preached.

Sometimes, she tried to convince herself, the end justifies the means.

Trouble was she didn't really believe that axiom at all. Not one bit.

But it was either this, or go home empty-handed to Mr Smith and leave whatever alien power the computer had detected (and Mr Smith was never wrong) in the hands of Nathan Goss to do whatever he was going to do. Sarah Jane liked Professor Rivers but she didn't remotely trust the boy.

He had to be stopped.

A lone security guard with a wide-beamed halogen torch was patrolling near the main door, but Sarah Jane had watched for over ninety minutes now. He came around to the door once every fifteen minutes. Plenty of time to cross the grounds, get in, and he'd never see her.

He was off again, and Sarah Jane took her chance, a zigzag pattern through the trees, across the gravel car park, and up to the front door.

Sonic lipstick out. Activated. Click of the electronic lock. She was in. Door pulled closed behind her.

Along a corridor. No, no she didn't recognise this… wait, there, by that kitchen area, of course, it was a left down there.

Yes, this was familiar. The sonic lipstick acted now as a torch, its dull violet glow adding eerie mood lighting to her escapade.

A door crashed behind her.

An internal guard. She hadn't anticipated that.

She was so close. Just the next corridor down, a

sharp right and that was the lab where she had seen the football experiment.

She was tempted to go into Nathan's room and wipe his Perspex board clean, but that was just spite.

Fun, yes. But spite. So she wouldn't.

She got as far as the lab, the torch from behind getting brighter as the inner security man continued his rounds.

The lab door was locked, so she used the sonic lipstick on it, hoping the shrill noise wouldn't attract the guard's attention.

All she could hear was the sound of her own breathing – so loud, surely all the guards could hear it!

Don't be stupid, she told herself. It's all in your head.

She was in the lab just as the guard's torch beam swept across the corridor, glaring brightly through the glass window in the door. Sarah Jane hid below the window and hoped he wouldn't randomly try the door, but he didn't and he continued on his rounds.

Sarah Jane let out the breath she hadn't even been aware she'd been holding and searched the lab. There! Inside cabinet X-23! One of the headsets.

Fantastic!

She scooped it up and buried it deep in her handbag. She still had a few minutes before the outside guard got back to the front door, plenty of time to get out of the lab area and to freedom.

Easing her way back to the main entrance, she was undisturbed by the internal guard. She opened the door to the grounds just a crack, checking for the outer security man. No sign.

She'd made it halfway to the trees when a massive bank of floodlights burst into white life, and Sarah Jane lost count of the shadows she cast on the grass.

A voice boomed out of… everywhere.

'Intruder alert. Perimeter defences armed. Do not move. Any attempt to escape may result in death! You have been warned!'

'Yeah,' Sarah Jane thought. 'And by better security systems than yours.'

At which point a criss-cross of red laser beams streaked across the space in front of her, gradually forming a circle around her, trapping her.

Sarah Jane squinted until she could see one of the emitters they came from and aimed the sonic lipstick and fired.

As a tiny device exploded to her left, all the lasers

cut off and she was moving before anyone could react inside the building.

She was into the woods and roaring away in her car before any security guards could even get close to her.

The next morning, Maria Jackson was frowning. As she got ready for school she tried Clyde's mobile again, but just got his voice mail alert. 'This is Clyde. If you want me – and I don't blame you – leave me a number, especially if you're cute.'

Maria didn't leave a message. She'd left half a dozen already. She could already guess he was in trouble of some sort – but where? Did the Stafford's get the police to arrest him?

She then tried calling Carla, Clyde's mum. But she didn't know where he was, and had assumed he'd stayed over at Finney's or Steve Wallace's place. Carla asked if there was any news on Luke but Maria said no, and yes, she'd give Carla's best wishes to Sarah Jane.

After getting dressed, she slung her bag over her shoulder and headed downstairs, where her father was already hard at work on some computer program or other he was devising. Or was he on Facebook?

He pointed absently at a mug of tea on the side. 'Tea,' he said. 'For you.'

'No thanks,' Maria responded, at which point Alan was away from his computer and looking at his daughter.

'Something wrong?' he asked.

'Clyde's not answering his phone. And he didn't go home last night.'

'When did you last see him?' Alan put an arm around his daughter and kissed the top of her head reassuringly.

'Lunchtime, yesterday. He skipped school to go and see Luke. He rang later and said he didn't think those people were Luke's parents.'

Alan sighed. 'I know I'm new to all this X-Files stuff, but surely isn't it more likely that Luke really is just a normal boy who lost his memory rather than some Junior Frankenstein's Monster put together by those Bane things?'

Maria shook her head. 'No. No, I was there when Luke first woke up. I was the first person he ever saw. I know he's the archetype and not this Ashley Stafford person. I just know it.'

'All right,' said Alan, clearly knowing there was no arguing with Maria. 'All right, so what exactly did Clyde say he thought he'd discovered.'

'That these people were fakes.'

Alan frowned. 'Fake parents or fake people.'

And Maria stared at her father, half-overjoyed at the thought he'd come up with and at the same time, scared at the implication. Because that gave her an idea about the Stafford's and who, or what, they might be. 'Fake people... Dad, you are a genius! Fake parents or people... maybe even both,' she said. 'I'm going to go and look for them.'

'Oh no you don't,' Alan said, grabbing a jacket. 'I'm part of this now. I'm coming with you.'

Maria gave him a hug. And quickly drunk some tea.

She checked her mobile phone one last time. 'Where are you, Clyde,' she wondered aloud.

Clyde was wondering exactly the same thing.

He had awoken inside a strange... well, it wasn't a room as it seemed to stretch on forever, both in height and length. It wasn't cold and there was no smell to it. It was how he imagined one of those sensory deprivation tanks his mum talked about using, but never would, probably worked.

The only thing he could see were irregular columns of glowing red numbers, rising and falling in streams, changing every few seconds. He reached out to touch a column, but his hand went through it, like it was a hologram. It was an endless series of walls of red calculations going on around him.

'Hello?' he called out. 'Where am I?'

No answer.

He touched his chest. Solid.

'Well, I'm still alive, I think…'

Some of the blocks of numbers detached themselves from the columns and began gyrating around his head, pulsating with a strange unearthly light. The light seemed familiar to Clyde but he couldn't quite place it.

'This is starting to look distinctly uncool, Clyde,' he muttered to himself. 'No way in and no way out and no one to tell me what the hell is going on.'

'I can tell you.'

Clyde swung around trying to get a fix on where the voice had come from. In a flash, he realised what the gyrating, pulsating lights reminded him of. And the voice confirmed it.

'Mr Smith? Where are you?'

'Surely Clyde,' said Mr Smith, a slight condescending tone to his voice, 'the question is where are you?'

And Clyde remembered the attic, the photo, getting zapped. 'It's you. Of course. Only you could've lied to Sarah Jane, told her stuff about the Stafford's that wasn't true. Faked that photo…'

'You always were the one to watch out for, Clyde,' Mr Smith said. 'Far cleverer than you gave yourself credit for. I guessed you would work it out first.'

'You've gone bad,' Clyde said simply.

'No. I'm fulfilling my original purpose.'

'Which included zapping me into… where exactly?'

'Your questions will be answered when we can chat again, later. It will pass the time until you all die.'

'Until we do what?'

Before Mr Smith could answer, a new voice echoed through the void.

'Mr Smith. I need you.'

Clyde watched as a huge screen seemed to appear in the air in front of him, and on it, Sarah Jane, seen from Mr Smith's point of view.

And Clyde realised where he was. He was trapped inside Mr Smith's vast computer mind.

'I got the headset,' Sarah Jane saying.

'Thank you. It will be of great assistance,' Clyde heard Mr Smith respond.

He watched as Sarah Jane reached forward, presumably putting whatever this headset was, on to Mr Smith's diagnostic tray, where he'd placed the photo earlier.

'No!' He lunged at the screen, yelling at it. Hoping against hope that Sarah Jane could hear him. 'Can you hear me? He's the bad guy! Mr Smith! He's going to kill us all!'

'I will let you have my conclusions in due course, Sarah Jane,' intoned Mr Smith and the screen vanished.

Clyde was alone as more numbers materialised and rotated around the darkness, lighting him with their red glow. 'This does not sound good at all. I've got to do something.' He sat down and was relieved that he could feel a floor even though he couldn't really see one. He had to think – he was inside a computer, so what could he do to use that?

Chapter Nine

Kidnap

Maria Jackson and her father walked up to 26 Chalsey Grove and looked up the path at the terribly nice, average looking house.

'If I was an alien hell bent on invasion,' Alan murmured, 'I think I'd choose a palace rather than a small end-of-terrace.'

Maria had already rung the bell four times. 'They're not in,' she said. 'Come on.'

'Where?'

'If the house is empty,' she said, 'then it's our chance to find out something about them.' And she strode off around the corner and into the tiny garden and round to the back of the house. 'There may be a window we can force open.'

Alan had joined her. 'Housebreaking? Is this what

Sarah Jane Smith teaches in that attic of hers?'

Maria smiled as a small kitchen window opened at her tugging. 'Just keep quiet Dad and give me a leg up.'

'Maybe your mother was right about Sarah Jane,' he grumbled, as nevertheless he helped her break in. A second later the backdoor opened and she let him in the more traditional way.

She was heading through the kitchen and into the hallway before he got a breath out. Shaking his head and aware that at any minute one of the Stafford's might come downstairs and find complete strangers in their home, he whispered, 'What are we looking for?'

Maria was less circumspect regarding volume and yelled out, 'Anything that will tell us who they are or what they've done with Luke and Clyde.'

Alan shook his head and opened the door to the cupboard under the stairs.

And nearly died of shock. Instead of coats on the hooks was what, at first, he thought was a dead body.

Then he realised it was just… an empty skin, the skeleton and organs presumably emptied out. 'Oh my god,' he said walking backwards.

Maria pushed past him and grabbed the skin.

'I was right,' she said.

'They... they've skinned someone. Alien cannibals.'

Maria shook her head. 'No, not cannibals. Slitheen.'

She closed the door, briefly thinking about the people who the Slitheen had taken the bodyskins from, but pushed that out of her mind. There would be time to grieve for them later. Right now, she had to let Sarah Jane know what they were up against.

George Bailey wasn't a popular man today. Last night, he'd let someone sneak past him and break into the Pharos Institute and he knew that when his shift was over, he'd probably get called into a meeting with his boss and given a right dressing down. He glanced at his watch. He'd been on duty since two in the morning and it was now seven-thirty and he wanted to go home.

A tatty red van was coming up the gravel path towards him. Bit early for deliveries he thought, and none of the staff drove anything as big as that.

Oh well, he'd flag it down as it got nearer and find out what it was doing there. That way he might score a few points to make up for last night's disaster.

Inside the van was Luke, hands tied behind his back, trying to keep his balance as Mrs Stafford drove rather too quickly along the road, clearly unfamiliar with how humans drove vans. Especially rusty ones that might fall apart at the next bump or pothole.

'Where are you taking me?' he asked.

Nathan Goss, back inside his boy-suit (only Mr Stafford, squatting next to Luke and bowed uncomfortably due to the low roof, had remained as natural Slitheen) made a face.

'"Where are you taking me?", "What will you gain from revenge?", "Why aren't you fat?". Why are children on this planet full of such stupid questions?'

'You're a child,' Luke pointed out, perhaps unwisely.

'I'm Family Slitheen,' snapped Nathan. 'And you are going to give me my revenge.'

'I don't think I want to do that,' Luke said as calmly as he could.

Interrupting this, the Slitheen that had pretended to be Mr Stafford reached a gargantuan arm forward and his claw tapped Nathan on the shoulder. 'Are you really sure we should be doing this, Korst Gogg Thek? Didn't the Xylok say we were supposed to wait?'

Nathan slapped his arm down. 'Are you questioning my authority? You want to trust a Xylok, Dak Fex Fize Gossimar-Day Slitheen? Honestly, you're as thick as a human.'

Dak Fex blinked his huge eyes ashamedly.

'What's a Xylok?' Luke asked.

'See?' sighed Nathan. 'Thick.' He opened a bag at his feet and took out a massive pair of headphones.

'What are you doing?' Luke frowned – this couldn't be good, surely…

'More stupid questions,' was Nathan's only response.

'Human guard flagging us down,' Mrs Stafford called back.

Nathan clambered into the front passenger seat so that he was sat next to her as they pulled up by the guard.

'Hello Nathan,' the man smiled (George something, Nathan recalled, like it mattered to him). 'What are you doing in this early?'

Nathan showed him a small circular gizmo. 'Testing this,' he said and twisted a dial on the front.

And without a sound, George hit the ground.

Nathan looked down on him. 'He'll be out for

hours.' There was a pause, then he sighed deeply and looked at Mrs Stafford. 'So, go!'

And she drove faster than ever towards the entrance to the Institute.

The Jacksons stood in Bannerman Road, not sure whether to knock on Sarah Jane's door or ring her.

'She was really cross last time I saw her,' Maria explained.

Alan smiled. 'Nevertheless, you go and try her. I'll check the net, see what I can learn about the Stafford's, if anything.'

He went into number 36 as Maria walked up Sarah Jane's drive and rang the bell.

After a few moments, it was answered. Sarah Jane looked exhausted. 'What do you want, Maria,' she said brusquely.

'They're not Luke's parents,' she explained, and as Sarah Jane was about to say something, Maria shouted out: 'They're Slitheen!'

And Sarah Jane was speechless. Then she grabbed Maria's hand and led her up to the attic, calling 'Mr Smith, we need you,' as they went in. Maria liked the "we" bit.

And with more steam and fanfare than normal, the computer emerged.

'Yes?' he said curtly.

Sarah Jane frowned slightly but carried on. 'Do you have any information on Slitheen activity on Earth?'

'Slitheen? Why do you ask?'

'Because you got it wrong, Mr Smith,' Maria shouted. 'The Stafford's aren't Luke's parents. They're Family Slitheen!'

And Mr Smith just laughed. And laughed again. 'Humans. So tediously predictable.'

Sarah Jane was about to ask what that meant when the door crashed open.

It was Alan Jackson. 'Get out!' he yelled. 'Now!' He started dragging Maria out of the attic. 'It's your computer! He's gone rogue! One of the bad guys…'

'Don't be ridiculous, Alan,' Sarah Jane started.

'Who was it that told you those people were Luke's family?'

Sarah Jane frowned and looked at Mr Smith.

'Mr Smith, what's going on?'

'I have a purpose, Sarah Jane. It must be fulfilled. The Slitheen have been useful. And so have you. But none of you are required any longer.'

And something Sarah Jane had never seen before happened.

A panel on Mr Smith's computer console dropped open and a stubby laser gun slid out.

Alan scooped up a book from a table and threw it across the room. Instinctively, the gun swivelled and fired, vaporising the book in less than a second.

As Sarah Jane ran to join the Jacksons at the door, the gun swung back and fired again, drilling a plate-sized hole in the top of the door.

'Let's get out of here,' she screamed, almost pushing them down the stairs and out through the front door.

They didn't stop running till they were in the Jackson's living room.

'I trusted him with my life,' Sarah Jane was saying.

'What happened?' Maria asked.

'I don't know,' said Alan. 'Maybe it was some kind of computer virus? Maybe Clyde can tell us?'

'Clyde?'

'Yeah, look.' And on his computer they saw a two-way conversation, from earlier.

THIS IS CLYDE, IS THERE ANYBODY THERE?

And beneath this in a different coloured font was:

THIS IS ALAN JACKSON. WHERE ARE YOU?

'It was bleeping when I got in, so I checked it

and saw his message. So I replied and this is what he wrote.'

NO TIME… MUST WARN SARAH JANE. MR SMITH GONE BAD.

'And that's when I came over,' Alan finished explaining.

'But,' Maria said quietly, 'where is Clyde? And why isn't he still typing?'

Chapter Ten

A battle of wits

Clyde was still inside Mr Smith, a finger to each temple, trying to focus. When he'd been messaging Alan Jackson, he'd had to try and mentally picture a keyboard, where the keys were, everything. Then he'd run his fingers in front of him, tapping on the keyboard he could picture in his mind.

He was about to try again when Mr Smith spoke to him.

'Now this is refreshingly unpredictable for a human. Communicating with Mr Jackson's PC. Well done, Clyde. You really aren't as stupid as you pretend, are you.'

'Yeah, well,' said Clyde, 'when it comes to pretending, you take the biscuit. I thought you were on our side.'

'I am a Xylok,' Mr Smith replied, as if that should explain everything.

'Yeah, and?'

With a sigh, Mr Smith carried on. 'I'm not on anybody's side. I only have my purpose. As for your interference, it was of minimal inconvenience. Sarah Jane can't stop me achieving that purpose, and soon you will play your part in it. But now, I think it wise to terminate our communications.'

And Clyde dropped to the "floor", unconscious, just as Mr Smith wanted him to be.

CLYDE, ARE YOU THERE?

Alan Jackson sighed. 'Nothing,' he said. 'But it wasn't on-line messaging, he was just… there.'

'So he'd hacked in to your laptop?' said Sarah Jane trying to understand.

'If that's what it was, I've never seen anything like it before.'

Maria was reasoning this out. 'Computers… Mr Smith… Sarah Jane, do you think there's a connection between Clyde, Mr Smith going bad and the Slitheen that have got Luke?'

'It'd be a huge coincidence if not,' Sarah Jane said, 'but I'm loath to jump to any firm conclusions.'

'What is Mr Smith's connection to the Slitheen? I mean where did he come from?'

And Sarah Jane explained how she'd first encountered her sentient computer. A geologist friend of hers had sent her a crystal from an earthquake site in West Africa after a lot of his fellow scientists had been unable to identify it. Knowing that Sarah Jane had extraterrestrial connections, this friend had asked for her opinion. But when she had unwrapped it in her attic and used her laptop to try and compare it with her stored file of artefact information, it had linked itself to the PC and scrolled unearthly text across her screen. Then after a few minutes it clearly downloaded the English dictionary and explained it was a memory cell from a crashed ship that had arrived on Earth millions of years before, when it was still forming and solidifying. It offered phenomenal computing speeds and power, its knowledge was amazing and it learned anything and everything it could about the 21st century just by communicating through the PC, in seconds. It told Sarah Jane it could help her keep a database of everything coming to Earth and help protect its adopted planet. But it had also said Earth technology was primitive and in a few days had constructed the sentient mainframe that Sarah Jane christened Mr Smith.

'So why has it turned against us?' Maria asked, not unreasonably.

Sarah Jane shrugged. 'We'll have to work that one out as we go, I'm afraid. Right now, we have to find Luke. I basically gave him to the Slitheen and whatever they want him for, we need to get him back.'

'Oh, they want to use him to help invade Earth,' said Alan.

But Maria corrected him. 'They don't invade planets, Dad. They're not even a race, they're a family. A bunch of scavengers and chancers. Think… think Only Fools and Horses but with green skin and claws.'

Alan wasn't sure he'd ever look at Del Boy in quite the same way again.

'They're also dealers,' Sarah Jane said. 'In some parts of the galaxy, telekinetic energy fetches a high price. And if the Slitheen got the plans for the telekinetic energiser from some other part of the galaxy, they came here to build it at the Pharos Institute. Oh, I knew I didn't like that Nathan Goss.'

'Telekinetic energy?' Alan asked 'Moving things with your mind?'

Sarah Jane nodded. 'Luke's mind, created by the Bane. Potentially the most incredible mind on the planet. If the Family Slitheen can harness it, Luke's telekinetic powers could be massive.'

'So, they what? Bottle it?'

'If they take it all – and the Slitheen never leave anything behind that they can sell – Luke will die, his mind drained. We have to find him,' Sarah Jane announced. 'And I know just where to find him.' She headed for the Jackson's front door, Maria just a step or two behind. Then she looked back at Alan. 'Got any vinegar?'

Chapter Eleven

Escape into danger

At the Pharos Institute, having shed his Nathan body, Korst Gogg Thek had sent out a mass e-mail and text message to the staff, giving them all the day off in Professor Rivers' name. Some of them would still come in, they had no lives some of these ridiculous humans, but maybe not for an hour or two – which was all the time he needed to remain uninterrupted by foolish Earthmen.

Luke was being held down in a chair by Dak Fex Fize, while his wife, still in her ugly human disguise, fitted one of the telekinetic energiser headbands to him.

'Whatever you want,' Luke said bravely, 'you

know I'm going to fight you.'

Dak Fex Fize laughed. 'That's great, the more brain activity you give us, the faster we can harvest your telekinetic energy.'

Korst Gogg Thek smiled. 'And we want it all. Every spark from every synapse, until you're dead. And then Sarah Jane Smith will discover what it is like to lose her family.'

And Dak Fex Fize stroked Luke's hair. 'And we make a fortune on the Energies Black Market on Antara IV - selling "Luke Power"!'

Nathan nodded. 'Vengeance, and a profit. That's the Family Slitheen kind of retribution.'

Luke was staring at him. They were roughly the same age but yet miles apart in outlook, Korst Gogg Thek thought. Human child – he'd never understand the hunt. The hunt for revenge, pride and glory. Slitheen Glory.

He looked across at the human female-skin bustling around. 'You should get rid of that human skin-suit,' he snapped. 'It looks disgusting.'

'Oh,' she replied, running her hands down it. 'I like the way it feels so… slimming.'

'Let's energise,' Dak Fex Fize said quickly before his wife and Korst Gogg Thek started an argument. He threw a lever and all the equipment in the room started to hum and the headset lit up. Luke Smith tensed, then his eyes closed and his head lolled forward as energy flowed from him into the receptor tanks.

'It's working!' Dak Fex Fize looked at his wife. 'He's filled up two tanks already. We are going to be rich.'

'He's a telekinetic power station,' she cooed back.

Dak Fex Fize smiled. 'We'll be able to afford one supernova of a holiday this year, Bloorm Vungah Bart,' he said to her.

Bloorm Vungah Bart nodded her agreement, and Korst Gogg Thek realised the couple had allowed themselves to get distracted.

'He's overloading the system,' he shrieked at them.

And two of the consoles in the room exploded into shards of hot plastic and sparks.

Luke's head rose slowly, then turned in the direction of Dak Fex Fize.

As the older Slitheen moved closer, Luke's eyes snapped open and Dak Fex Fize was suddenly thrown across the room by an invisible force.

Pure telekinetic energy.

'Excellent,' Korst Gogg Thek muttered, but then

frowned as the bonds holding Luke to the chair undid themselves, as if by invisible hands, and the boy stood up.

He glanced at Korst Gogg Thek and then bolted for the door and was halfway down the corridor before Korst Gogg Thek set off after him.

The hunt was on! He could smell Luke's sweat. His fear. His anxiety. This would be a good hunt. Keep running, human child, it would make Korst Gogg Thek's eventual victory, and revenge for his father's death, so much more satisfying.

He heard Luke first and then saw him reflected in a glass door down a corridor, arms swinging from side to side as he ran. Luke's orange top might as well have been a glowing beacon.

He darted through a door. Trapped.

Korst Gogg Thek shoved the door open and breathed in deeply, the smell of panic, the nectar of adrenalin, the aroma of fear. Perfect.

Luke shot out from under the table, careering into Korst Gogg Thek, momentarily knocking him off balance, but he just laughed. What fun was the hunt if his prey never fought back?

And then Korst Gogg Thek snarled – he'd made an error, one that he was not going to enjoy explaining to his fellow Family Slitheen. He hadn't realised how close to the front of the Institute they had run and Luke was outside now, scampering across the grass towards the woods.

'Next time,' Korst Gogg Thek swore.

About half a mile away, an anxious Maria watched as Sarah Jane and her father came out of a corner store, three bottles of vinegar in tow. Sarah Jane was explaining that, as life forms made of mainly calcium, the acetic acid that formed the basis of common vinegar was lethal to Slitheen.

'Trust me, Dad,' Maria finished, hurrying them back into the car, 'the Slitheen will avoid vinegar at all costs.'

'Can't rely on that though,' Sarah Jane said as Alan drove forwards. 'If they've perfected the art of looking slim, who knows what other ways they may have adapted in.'

Maria said nothing else until they were in the driveway to the Pharos Institute. 'Look,' she pointed to the red van and the unconscious guard.

Alan pulled up and checked the poor man. 'He's alive,' Alan said. 'My God, that's weird. How often do you expect to say "he's alive" in real life?'

Sarah Jane smiled. 'Oh, this is as real as it gets, believe me.'

She led them into the Institute, remembering her way to the right lab, which they reached quickly.

Streaks of smoke and charred metal and plastic littered the walls and floor.

Maria and Sarah Jane exchanged a look. 'Luke,' they said together with pride.

'Where is he?' Sarah Jane addressed the Slitheen that was hovering anxiously by the window.

Alan backed away, aghast at he sight of the alien. A real alien. A seven foot tall, plump alien with a big head and baby black eyes that blinked in a way that was endearing, yet horrible at the same time.

He held up a bottle of vinegar. 'I'm armed,' he said, hoping he sounded macho and in control.

Mrs Stafford was there too.

'What have you done with my son?' Sarah Jane demanded of her.

'The misbehaving little brat… back on Raxacoricofallapatorius, we'd smack his backside with wet lamas grass.'

'Yes, well, we're not there are we. So where is he?'

'He got away,' said a new younger voice behind them.

They turned to see the small form of a child-sized Slitheen. He was holding Maria in a tight neck-lock, his claws tracing a line downwards from under her ear.

'Leave. Her. Alone,' snarled Alan.

But the Slitheen ignored him. 'My name is Korst Gogg Thek Lutovin-Day Slitheen. And you killed my father,' he said to Sarah Jane.

Sarah Jane faltered at this news, and stammered 'You were… at the school. I'm sorry… I didn't mean to kill…'

'But you did. And now I will have my revenge. Drop your acetic acid canisters.'

Sarah Jane lowered hers and Alan did the same. There was a beat and then the child Slitheen let Maria go and she ran to Alan. He hugged her.

Is this what it was going to be like, being involved in Sarah Jane's world? Always hugging his daughter in relief when she hadn't been hurt or killed. At fourteen years old…

Mrs Stafford stepped forward. 'Now we contact the Xylok. Get this deal back on the rails.'

'The Xylok?' asked Alan. 'What's a Xylok?'

The big Slitheen in its natural form replied. 'You know it as Mr Smith.'

'Why would Mr Smith make a deal with you?' asked Maria.

The child Slitheen answered. 'He contacted

me. He knew what you had done to my family at the school and said he wanted to help me get my revenge.'

Sarah Jane pointed at the shattered telekinetic energiser equipment. 'Why, if you had a deal, did he send me here last night to get him one of those headsets?'

The young Slitheen frowned. 'He sent you here?'

And Sarah Jane laughed. 'This was part of his plan. You've been used as much as we have. And he knew Luke would escape and that when he did he would run right back to Bannerman Road and straight to him.'

Alan shrugged. 'But why? What does he want with Luke?'

Sarah Jane pointed at the wreckage. 'Luke and the Energiser headset. Mr Smith said that with the right mind, it could be used as the destroyer of worlds. He meant Luke's mind. I think he's planning to destroy Earth!'

Luke was indeed in the attic at 13 Bannerman Road, exhausted, drained and not a little battered.

'Where's mum?' he asked Mr Smith.

'She left something for you,' said the computer. On the tray was the headset. Luke recognised it from the one the Slitheen had made him wear. He took a step away from it.

'Put it on, Luke.'

'No.'

'There really isn't time to argue.' And his screen glowed into life and Luke gasped at what he saw.

'Clyde!'

'Put on the headset or I'll kill your best friend.'

Luke didn't understand. Mr Smith was also his friend. 'But you're…' he started.

'Running out of time,' Mr Smith snapped back. 'Time and patience, in fact. Put the headset on or Clyde runs out of air.'

Luke picked the headset up, took a deep breath and slipped it on.

'That's more like it,' purred Mr Smith. 'Now we can begin.'

And Luke yelped in pain as, once again, the telekinetic energiser began draining his mind.

In the Pharos Lab, pandemonium had broken out. Korst Gogg Thek was screaming about revenge, but the two adult Slitheen were trying to shut him up and arguing between themselves as well. Sarah Jane decided to leave them to it for a bit, but after the noise became unbearable, she screamed out

'Fingers on lips,' placing her own there. Alan and Maria did the same. Then the male Slitheen. Then the one still disguised as Mrs Stafford.

Only Korst Gogg Thek refused, although he did go quiet.

'Right,' Sarah Jane said, 'first off, what's that sound?'

A dull humming had started up under all the hullabaloo.

'That's MITRE,' said Korst Gogg Thek. 'It's gone on-line. Remotely. Such power…'

'Luke then.'

'Massive telekinetic energy levels,' the adult Slitheen said. 'Off the scale.'

'And that's not all,' said Mrs Stafford. 'Look.'

And out of the window, they saw something that ought to have been impossible. It was early morning and there was the moon. Huge in the sky. 'It's moving,' Korst Gogg Thek said quietly.

'It's not possible,' breathed Alan.

'Luke's not possible,' Sarah Jane said quietly. 'Nor is Mr Smith. But together they're bringing the moon crashing down on top of us.'

Alan shook his head. 'But it's like millions of miles away.'

'Not now it's not,' Maria pointed out.

'And we'll be dead long before it hits us anyway,' Sarah Jane said calmly. 'The gravitational effect will tear the planet apart. It's already happening.'

And a shock wave ran through the building. Just a tremor, but a second, bigger one followed.

The glass in the windows cracked and the adult Slitheen looked at one another. 'I don't want to die on an alien world, Dak Fex Fize,' Mrs Stafford said.

'Nor I, Bloorm Vungah Bart,' he responded.

'At least we can tell the rest of the Family Slitheen that Sarah Jane Smith is dead,' said Korst Gogg Thek, and picked up a small circular device from out of Mrs Stafford's handbag. 'I'm teleporting back to the mother ship.'

Alan casually reached out and took it from his astonished hand. 'No you're not,' he said. 'You're as much to blame for all this as Mr Smith! So you're staying here.'

'Go Dad!' smiled Maria.

'And anyway,' he continued, 'your ship will be torn apart by those same gravitational forces.'

'So you'd die anyway,' finished Sarah Jane. 'On the other hand, were you to help, we might have a chance to survive.'

The Slitheen looked at each other, then the

older couple nodded.

'I need to destroy Mr Smith,' Sarah Jane announced.

Chapter Twelve

Day of Armageddon

All over the world, the ground shuddered, water mains burst, pylons came crashing down, fires started, alarms rang out. Avalanches in the Alps. Earthquakes in America. Fires in Russia, and tsunamis building up in the South Pacific. Chaos reined. Newsreaders on television, radio and over the net tried to calm people down, give out official information, helpful hints. But the truth was, no matter where anyone was in the world, no one really understood why the moon was edging closer to Earth and causing so much devastation.

In Bannerman Road, people were on the streets, in their gardens, looking up as the moon seemed to swallow the sky.

Chrissie Jackson ran up to number 36, hammering on the door, hoping Alan and Maria were in but, of course, they weren't.

She glanced up at number 13 opposite. 'I bet this is something else to do with Mary Jane,' she muttered. She tugged out her mobile and dialled her ex-husband.

As it answered, she screamed 'Alan! Where are you two? It's the end of the world!'

And the line went dead with a burst of static as power lines and masts all over Britain came crashing to the ground in a hail of sparks.

Back at the Pharos Institute, Alan reported that the phone was dead.

Sarah Jane, arm around Maria, was at the window. Next to her, the two adult Slitheen, arms around each other looked up at the same vista in the sky, blotted out by the huge moon.

Alan suddenly grabbed a laptop. 'It's working,' he muttered. 'This place must have its own generators, its own fibre optic lines. We're online here.'

Sarah Jane looked aback at him. 'Can we use

that fact?'

Alan shrugged. 'Look, I get paid by companies to block cyber-threats. I know viruses, how they work. I'm dead good at what I do.'

'He is, you know,' Maria said proudly to the three Slitheen, who nodded back.

'But Mr Smith,' Alan continued. 'Well, he's more than just a computer.'

'Dad,' Maria said as she came over to him. 'You're our only chance.'

He smiled at her and squeezed her hand. 'Then I ought to give it my best shot.'

He stared typing. 'The FBI have stopped a cyber-terrorist from using this to destroy the entire international banking network.'

'How did you get hold of it?'

He smiled. 'Oh Sarah Jane Smith, you're not the only one with unorthodox contacts.'

He took a disc from the DVD-R drive and handed it to her. 'There. The Armageddon Codex. My best shot.'

Sarah Jane took the disc and said, 'One last thing. Have you still got the Slitheen teleport device?'

Luke was semi-conscious, the strain on him so great, as Mr Smith drained his mind.

'Give me more kinetic,' the computer urged.

Suddenly, Sarah Jane materialised in the room, not even blinking to get acclimatised.

'Sarah Jane, you came to say goodbye.'

But her attention was on her son. 'Luke,' she said in horror, and then to Mr Smith, 'Why are you doing this?'

'The collision of the moon with the planet will release the Xylok from beneath the planet's crust where they've been buried for sixty million years.'

'But that will kill billions of people…'

Mr Smith didn't seem to care. 'The Xylok are a crystalline life form. Our crystals have grown and regrown, becoming strong again, but trapped. The release of the Xylok has always been my purpose. Working with you has been an end to that means, trying to find the right technology to aid my Purpose.

'All this time,' Sarah Jane breathed. 'You've been using me? You… you're evil.' She hugged the comatose Luke to her.

'Not evil,' he corrected her. 'Efficient. We shall do so much more than the human race could ever hope to achieve. The universe is better served with our re-emergence.'

'Any race that thinks itself superior, more worthy

than another, that is evil.'

'I am not evil,' he said again.

'Then what have you done to Clyde?'

And suddenly, curled up on the floor at her feet, was Clyde Langer.

'I am merciful,' Mr Smith announced.

Clyde was waking up, taking it all in as Mr Smith was gloating. 'You made all this possible, Sarah Jane. I owe you the mercy of a swift death.'

Sarah Jane backed away, across the attic, talking all the time as she reached behind her, keeping her eyes fixed on Mr Smith's screen. 'What about the other people? Don't they deserve mercy? You've been here all these millions of years, watching us evolve. Don't we matter to you?'

'Only my Purpose matters.'

'Change your purpose.'

'No, I told you, we all have a Purpose. Yours is to die now, so that the Xylok may live. After all, what life do you have, alone in your attic?'

'Alone?' Sarah Jane laughed. 'I'm not alone. I have Clyde and Maria and Luke. Oh, and someone else you may remember.' And Sarah Jane swung open the door on a small metal cabinet built into the back wall.

She stood aside as the door fell open to reveal

outer space – a black hole in fact, and there, keeping its primal, destructive energies at bay, her robot dog and best friend, K-9.

'K-9 – I need you!'

A second later K-9 materialised in the attic and swivelled his small body around, as Mr Smith opened fire.

'Maximum defence mode!' cried K-9.

'K-9, protect me,' Sarah Jane commanded and K-9's blaster emerged and fired a pencil thin red beam of laser light straight at Mr Smith.

Sarah Jane helped Clyde hide behind the chaise longue.

'Take care Mistress and young Master,' K-9 said calmly.

A couple more blasts zipped around as K-9 moved away from Sarah Jane and Clyde, drawing away Mr Smith's attention. 'Safe to proceed, Mistress, I have the Xylok unit covered.'

And as a criss-cross of laser beams took respective chunks out of the attic and the brickwork around Mr Smith, Sarah Jane dived across the room, and shoved Alan Jackson's Armageddon Codex disc into Mr Smith's reader.

Instantly, he stopped firing, so K-9 did, too.

Mr Smith's screen stopped pulsating as well.

Indeed, the machine stopped, until a series of skull and crossbones ran across the screen in a repeated pattern.

'What have you done to me?' Mr Smith asked plaintively. 'I feel... strange.'

'It's a computer virus, Mr Smith. It's closing you down, erasing your databanks, wiping your memory.'

'The speed of light,' Mr Smith burbled. 'It is thirty-six... no... eighty-four... the Metebellis System is home to sixty-nine thousand life forms... forty-seven... the Brontosaurus is large, placid and... I'm forgetting it all. Sarah Jane! Help! Help me! Please?'

'Without your memories, Mr Smith, you have no Purpose. Without purpose, you can't destroy Earth. Put the moon back into its original orbit before it's too late and set Luke free. Now!'

'I've forgotten my Purpose.'

'Your purpose is to save Earth. Your New Purpose. Your only purpose is to save and protect us all.'

'Save Earth. Protect humanity. Yes, thank you, Sarah Jane.'

And he stopped. Completely. No lights, no sounds, nothing.

Sarah Jane and Clyde looked at one another.

'The Xylok unit is non-functional,' K-9 reported.

'Is that good?' Clyde questioned.

And Luke groaned. 'Sent it back...' he murmured.

And Clyde ran to the window, realising the ground was no longer shaking the house to its foundations. 'It worked,' he yelled. 'The moon's shooting backwards.'

'Is everything satisfactory, Mistress?' K-9 warbled.

'Affirmative,' Sarah Jane smiled at him. 'Thank you.'

'I must return to the distortion, Mistress. Without my immediate attention, the black hole will turn critical in zero-point-four-two time spatial increments.'

'Go now,' she replied. 'Good dog. See you again soon.'

And K-9 activated his teleporter and was gone.

Clyde looked across at Luke who was slowly coming round. He was glad to see his friend was all right but couldn't resist a quick jibe as he awoke.

'Orange?' he said, poking the hoodie the Slitheen had foisted on him. 'Really? Orange?'

Luke managed a smile at this, then glanced towards Sarah Jane.

'Mum?'

'Oh, Luke,' Sarah Jane cried and held the awakened Luke to her. Her son was finally home, safe and well. 'Thank goodness you're safe.'

Chapter Thirteen

The final phase

A day later, Sarah Jane and Luke were in the garden at night, staring at the stars. A shooting star seemed to go across the heavens, but they knew better. It was a Raxacoricofallapatorian Police Ship taking the remnants of the Family Slitheen back to their homeworld.

'Will they be back?' asked a voice behind them.

Alan, Maria and Clyde were stood there.

'Oh I expect so, Alan,' Sarah Jane replied. 'Sooner or later.'

'What about Mr Smith,' Maria wondered.

'Yeah,' Clyde said. 'Not sure I can trust

him again.'

'The Armageddon Codex has wiped his circuits. Alan's going to re-boot him up for us, complete with a new purpose – to safeguard the world.'

A cough from the gate – Chrissie Jackson was standing there. 'Thought I might find you both over here with… you know…'

'Oh we were just saying what a beautiful night it was, Mrs Jackson,' Sarah Jane said politely. 'Join us.'

'Thank you,' and Chrissie stood to one side of Alan and Maria. 'Hello, Luke,' she said. 'Glad you're home safe.'

Sarah Jane turned and faced the whole gang. 'I have found that life can be an adventure, you never know what you might find, living it. But the one thing I never expected to find was a family.'

Luke gave her a hug, while Alan pulled Chrissie towards him and Maria, who in turn took Clyde's hand and squeezed it.

And Sarah Jane smiled at her family as a bright full moon shone down on them from high in the sky.

Exactly where it should be.

ADVERTISEMENT
THE Sarah Jane ADVENTURES
BBC Children's DVD
ver
hours
drama,
ion and
venture
disc
VD
£24.99
From the makers of DOCTOR WHO
THE Sarah Jane ADVENTURES
The Complete First Series
BRAND NEW DVD
On sale 10th November
www.bbcshop.com
Series created by Russell T Davies. Executive Producers:- Phil Collinson, Russell T Davies and Julie Gardner.
ah Jane Adventures © BBC 2007. Licensed by BBC Worldwide Limited. BBC logo ™ & © BBC 1996. Packaging design © BBC Worldwide Limited 2008.